THE UNOFFICIAL

MINECRAFT™ TOOL KIT

SKY'S THE LIMIT
WITH MINECRAFT™

JOEY DAVEY   JONATHAN GREEN   JULIET STANLEY

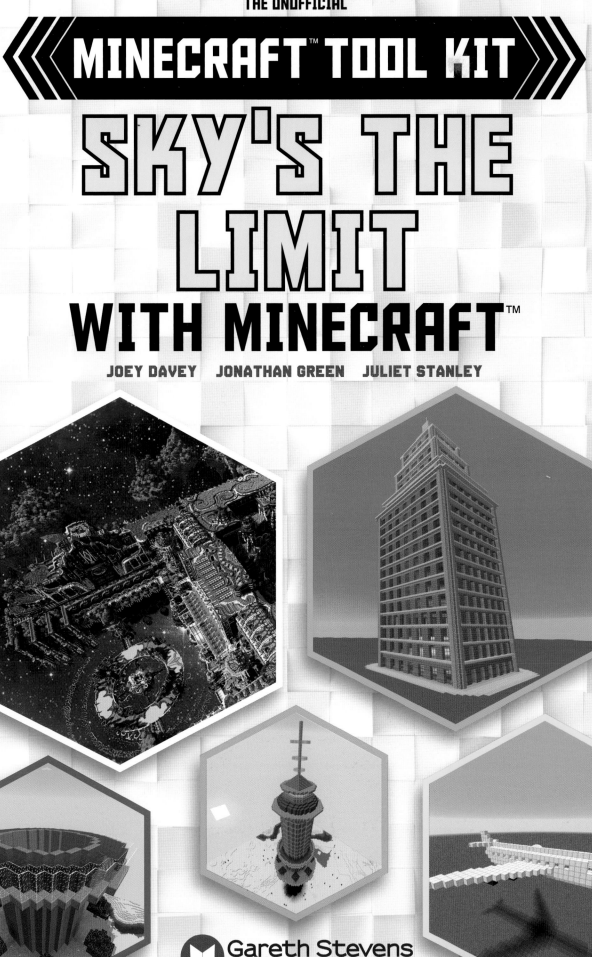

Gareth Stevens
PUBLISHING

Please visit our website, **www.garethstevens.com**.
For a free color catalog of all our high-quality books,
call toll free 1-800-542-2595 or fax 1-877-542-2596.

Cataloging-in-Publication Data
Names: Davey, Joey. | Green, Jonathan. | Stanley, Juliet.
Title: Sky's the limit with Minecraft™ / Joey Davey, Jonathan Green, and Juliet Stanley.
Description: New York : Gareth Stevens Publishing, 2018. |
Series: The unofficial Minecraft™ tool kit | Includes index.
Identifiers: LCCN ISBN 9781538217153 (pbk.) | ISBN 9781538217108 (library bound) |
ISBN 9781538217054 (6 pack)
Subjects: LCSH: Minecraft (Game)--Juvenile literature. | Minecraft (Video game)--
Handbooks, manuals, etc.--Juvenile literature. |
Classification: LCC GV1469.M55 D38 2018 | DDC 794.8--dc23

Published in 2018 by
Gareth Stevens Publishing
111 East 14th Street, Suite 349
New York, NY 10003

Designed and packaged by: Dynamo Limited
Built and written by: Joey Davey, Jonathan Green, and Juliet Stanley

Printed in the United States of America
CPSIA compliance information: Batch CW18GS: For further information contact
Gareth Stevens, New York, New York at 1-800-542-2595.

CONTENTS

WELCOME
TO THE WONDERFUL WORLD OF
MINECRAFT!

If you're reading this, then you're probably already familiar with the fantastic game of building blocks and going on adventures. If you're not, go download Minecraft now and try it out!

READY?

OKAY, LET'S GET STARTED!

Courtesy of IAmNewAsWell

» THE AIM OF THE GAME «

One of the greatest things about Minecraft – apart from being able to explore randomly generated worlds – is that you can build amazing things, from the simplest home to the grandest castle. This book will help you become a master builder, capable of building your own epic Minecraft masterpieces.

This book has projects of three different difficulty ratings, which will help you hone your building skills. Each project has clear step-by-step instructions. You'll also find expert tips, like this one . . .

Courtesy of crpeh

EXPERT TIP!

CREATIVE MODE vs SURVIVAL MODE

If you build in Creative mode, you'll have all the blocks you need to complete your build, no matter how outlandish. However, if you like more of a challenge, why not build in Survival mode? Just remember – you'll have to mine all your resources first, and you will also be kept busy crafting weapons and armor to fend off dangerous mobs of zombies and creepers!

FAIL TO PREPARE AND PREPARE TO FAIL

If you're building in Survival mode, before you get going, you'll need to set up your hotbar so that items such as torches, tools, and weapons are all within easy reach. You'll also want to make sure that you're building on a flat surface.

For the best results, use Minecraft PC to complete all of the step-by-step builds in this book.

Before you start, you'll need to mine all your resources, and before you can do that, you'll need to sort out your Tool Kit . . . turn the page for further help.

Courtesy of swifsampson

EXPERT TIP!

ALL THAT GLITTERS

If you're planning on creating a Minecraft masterpiece, you'll want some super-special materials. To find rare ores, like diamonds, mine a staircase to Level 14 and then strip-mine the area. But remember – you'll need an iron or diamond pickaxe to mine most ores. If you use any other type of tool, you'll destroy the block without getting anything from it.

Courtesy of Cornbass

STAYING SAFE ONLINE

Minecraft is one of the most popular games in the world, and you should have fun while you're playing it. However, it is just as important to stay safe when you're online.

Top tips for staying safe are:
》 turn off chat
》 find a kid-friendly server
》 watch out for viruses and malware
》 set a game-play time limit
》 tell a trusted adult what you're doing

TOOLED UP!

Before you get cracking – or should that be crafting? – you're going to need to make sure that you're set with all the tools you'll need.

⟪ CUSTOMIZE YOUR HOTBAR ⟫

Your inventory is the place where everything you mine and collect is stored. You can access it at any time during the game.

When you exit your inventory, a hotbar will appear at the bottom of the screen, made up of a line of nine hotkey slots. Think of this as your mini-inventory where you can keep the things you use most frequently.

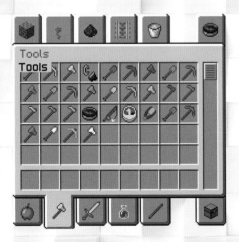

It's vitally important to take time to organize your hotbar carefully – in a game of Survival, it might just save your life!

Move an item from your inventory into one of the hotkey slots to assign it. Then, when you select a slot, the item you have placed in there will automatically appear in your hand, ready for you to use.

⟪ HOT OR NOT ⟫

Always keep at least one weapon and one food source in your hotbar. Also make sure you've got some tools in there. It's always handy to have a pickaxe or two, or perhaps a shovel, depending on what you're planning on mining. A torch will also be handy. Last of all, you want to make sure that you have some basic building materials ready.

EXPERT TIP!

GO FISH!

Fishing rods are surprisingly useful. You can use them to catch fish, and you can also cast them to set off pressure plates while you stay out of harm's way.

« BUILDING BLOCKS »

WOOD

Always useful, as you need it to craft many everyday items. In Survival mode, always carry some logs with you – especially if you're going caving, as wood is hard to find underground.

EXPERT TIP!

REDSTONE RAMPAGE

If you want your Minecraft masterpiece to have moving mechanisms, like a roller coaster, you're going to need some redstone. This block allows you to create moving parts, and even circuits.

STONE

The most common block in the game, it is good at keeping creepers at bay. If you're planning on building a castle, stone is what you're going to need – and lots of it!

BRICK

Harder than stone and can be crafted out of clay, although it does take a long time to craft and will drain your fuel supply.

OBSIDIAN

Other than bedrock, this is the hardest material – and it's completely creeper-proof! You'll need an entire lava source block and 15 seconds with a diamond pick to mine it in Survival mode, though.

« MIND-BOGGLING BIOMES »

The different types of terrain you encounter in Minecraft are called biomes. They range from ice plains and swamps, to deserts and jungles, to oceans and fantasy islands.

Courtesy of Epic Minecraft Seeds

Courtesy of MADbakamono

These biomes will take you to the sky and back, quite literally!

UN-BOX YOUR BUILD

The amazing world of Minecraft is made from lots and lots of . . . blocks! But these simple, straight-edged blocks certainly don't stop its biggest fans from building masterpieces that curve, spiral, and defy the cuboid. With a little help and a lot of imagination, you can make even your wildest dream builds come true. Let's take a look at some of the creative possibilities Minecraft has to offer.

≪ ECCENTRIC ENTRANCES ≫

Make your entrances unforgettable with lots of different materials, shapes, and a few surprises! The first door is the perfect entrance for a treetop lodge. From a distance it looks like it has been carved out of a tree trunk by woodland creatures. There's a hidden entrance in the second doorway, and the colors created by wool and emerald blocks are totally wild!

≪ WOW FACTOR WINDOWS ≫

Why not try your hand at making these stunning windows? Short rows, L-shapes, and single blocks create a circular web within the frame of the first window. Diagonally placed blocks in the second window create curved lines that look like a propeller. But you don't have to stick to square windows – anything is possible in Minecraft!

EXPERT TIP!

SKETCH IT

Being prepared will make building in Minecraft easier and much more fun. You'll have a good idea of what you want your final build to look like, and you'll have given yourself time to think about how to do it. Forget math for a second – grid paper is perfect for planning what to do with all of these blocks!

The dark blue flooring and back wall cleverly disguise this open entrance.

≪ REMARKABLE ≫ ROOFS

Here are three in-spire-ational roofs for you to try! For a look inspired by ancient Chinese architecture, add blocks in the corners of simple roof structures. Or go for a space age design with lava, emerald, diamond, and beacon blocks! Staying hidden is always a good strategy in Survival mode – this last grass roof is the perfect way to disguise your builds.

≪ SENSATIONAL ≫ STRUCTURES

Yes, it's a woolly hat house made from wool blocks! Try recreating this circular structure with lots of different-sized rows. The only rule is: stay symmetrical. This arched bridge is a super-simple structure, and it can be used to add interest to the front of a building, or to un-box square windows. The last building uses columns to support a balcony and to add texture to its surface. This would be a great look for a castle.

EXPERT TIP!

BE INSPIRED

Search online or flip through books to find inspiration for your creations! As well as a myriad of Minecraft buildings, you'll find plenty of weird and wonderful real-life buildings that you can use to help you come up with your very own masterpiece. Happy building, Minecrafters!

FLYING HIGH

Surely there can be nothing more stunning than a building floating high in the sky among the Minecraft clouds?

If you want to let your imagination take flight and craft your next incredible build far above Overworld, here's what you need to know . . .

« FLOATING ON AIR »

One of the weird but wonderful things about Minecraft is that the game allows for floating blocks – you simply place a block on the ground, then another one on top of it, remove the one on the bottom and – presto! – a floating block! If you're planning a sky build in Survival mode, start by making a staircase out of blocks of easy-to-find material like dirt or cobblestone. If you make your staircase six blocks high, you will be able to add blocks while you're still standing on the ground. You can protect yourself from hostile mobs by putting a fence around your stairs, but don't forget a gate for ease of access.

EXPERT TIP!

VANTAGE POINT

You can build a sky base anywhere there's open air – of course! – but it is to your advantage to have an area of flat ground underneath, as this makes it easier for you to check out your surroundings before descending to ground level. Alternatively, you could build over a lake to minimize the damage to yourself should you happen to fall.

EXPERT TIP!

SNEAKY

When building in the sky, it's worth remembering that if you hold down the Shift key, you can enter Sneak mode. This allows you to move out onto the edges of a block without falling off.

CASTLES IN THE CLOUDS

If you want to build higher up, it's a good idea to construct a platform to work from. Build your platform out from your staircase, making sure that it is at least three blocks wider than the foundation for your build. Add fence around the edge of your platform and you will have a safe walkway around your build during construction.

EXPERT TIP!

SAND IS BANNED

When you are building in the sky, some materials are better than others. If you want to use sand or gravel, make sure they don't form the bottom layer of your construction as they will fall if the blocks underneath them are removed.

EXPERT TIP!

BE PREPARED

You'll want to gather your resources before you start building in the sky. For this reason, it's easier to build a floating base after you've spent some time mining. Other useful items to craft before you start your Survival sky build include ladders and trapdoors.

THE SKY'S THE LIMIT

There are many advantages to building in the sky. You get a great view of your surroundings for a start, plus your build is safe from monster mobs, so you won't have any zombies or creepers troubling you at night. But most of all, your build will look out of this world!

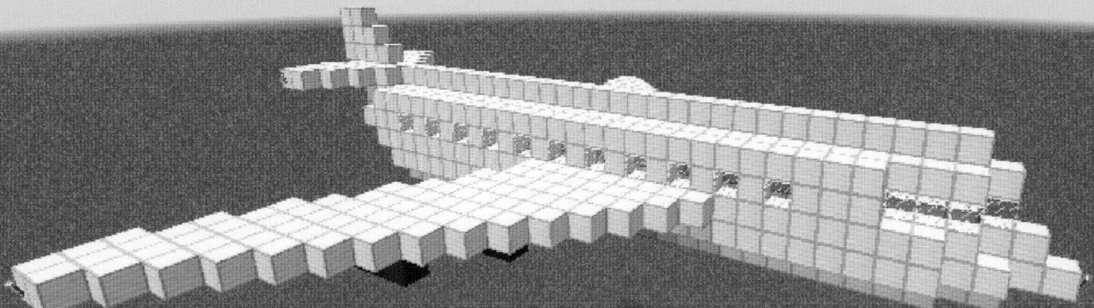

SKY'S THE LIMIT

PLANE »

DIFFICULTY
EASY

TIME
1 HOUR

It's not just buildings you can construct in Minecraft, and with that in mind, it's time to create your very own plane. Start by building a single-block stack from iron – go as high as you dare! – and then craft your plane on top of this. Once you've finished, you can remove the stack, jump on board, and survey the world from above. It's a great way to see your enemies coming in Survival mode.

MATERIALS

End 1

End 2

STEP 1

Build the plane's base from 26x5 iron blocks, adding seven blocks at End 1 and four at End 2. Underneath, add 26x3 blocks with two blocks at End 1 and one at End 2. Underneath that, build a 26-block row.

STEP 2

Build up the tail on top of End 1, as shown in these two images.

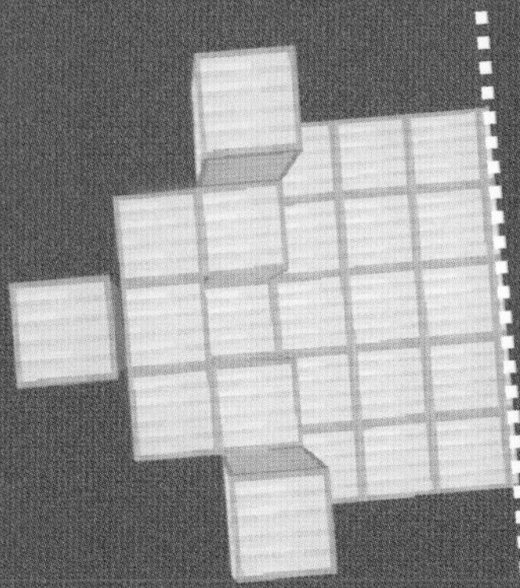

STEP 3

Add the tail at End 1. Build the tail fin, making sure it narrows to one block wide and steps up, as shown.

STEP 4

Now start work on the body of the plane. Build a 3-block L-shape on either side and place another block on the inside of the tail. This should be placed four blocks up, as shown in red.

STEP 5

Build the sides of your plane four blocks high, with gaps for windows and doors. Add a roof with a central row on top to form an aerodynamic spine. Finally, build tailplanes on each side of the tail, as shown.

STEP 6

At the front, build up from End 2 and extend the roof across and down to form the nose of the plane. Add glass for the windshield (and fill in all the window gaps with glass too) and pop a torch at the front as a light. Now it's time to build the wings . . .

STEP 7

Behind your second window, build a nine-block row along the side of your plane. Then add blocks in a staggered pattern to create your wings, as shown. Add jet engines from cyan hardened clay under each wing.

EXPERT TIP!

TAKE OFF!

Build an airport and runway to go with your plane. Use iron and glass for the airport and stone brick slab for the runway, with plenty of torches along the sides to make it visible from far away.

SKY'S THE LIMIT

SKY FORTRESS

DIFFICULTY
INTERMEDIATE

BUILD TIME
2 HOURS

This sky fortress is the perfect place to take stock before your next adventure in Survival mode. Before you start, you will need to build a single column of blocks up to the height you'd like your fortress to float at, or you could craft some steps up to it. Whatever you decide, make sure that you protect yourself from hostile mobs with tight security at ground level.

MATERIALS

STEP 1

Build a single layer of 21 emerald blocks, as pictured, and then surround it with three layers of stone blocks. Add a larger ring of stone blocks on the outside of the top row and build it up three blocks high, as shown here.

STEP 2

Join a wider ring joined to the top layer and build this up so it is four blocks high. Then add a two-block-high ring around the top of this until you have a structure like this one.

STEP 3

Add four more layers on top of your last layer. Keep your long sides five blocks wide, adding more blocks to each corner, as shown.

STEP 4

Now build eight-block-high walls up from the last layer, using emerald block for the seventh block up for decoration, as shown. One block inside these walls, build your walls another four blocks higher.

EXPERT TIP!

HIGH CLIMBER

Make a ladder shaft inside your sky fortress by building a small hollow column of blocks with a ladder going up one wall. No matter which key you press in a ladder shaft, you will move upwards, making it a great way to go up in the world!

STEP 5

At the bottom of your base, add a five-block emerald cross to the center of your emerald floor. Extend this down four layers and add a 14-block emerald column. Add rings of green stained glass block, as shown, for decoration.

STEP 6

Back at the top of your build, add a roof of iron block one layer down. On the same level, build a stone ring as shown here on the right.

STEP 7

Join your ring and fortress with grass blocks. Grow eight trees with saplings and bonemeal and add flowers, sheep, and pigs. Add a two-block-high inner wall. You should also add a wall around the outer edge to keep the animals from falling off!

STEP 8

Build the inner wall 20 blocks higher. Add a glass block ledge with stone edges 15 blocks up. Build three-block-high glass walls up from this edge and fill the gap between the inner stone walls and the outer glass walls with water.

STEP 9

Add another ring of stone blocks on top of your glass walls. Then build your inner walls another 29 blocks higher – you're literally reaching for the stars with this cloud-clipping sky fortress!

Three blocks up from the waterline, replace a layer with gray stained glass. Repeat this every fourth row and add glowstone block inside the fortress to provide light. Build your walls eight blocks higher, and then add four layers increasing in size at the top, as shown.

EXPERT TIP!

SAFE HAVEN

Surround ground-level access to your sky fortress with plenty of torches to stop hostile mobs spawning. Then build a simple gatehouse around your steps, with a water pit trap in front of the door to catch out creepers and all their horrible friends.

STEP 11

Fill in the top layer with stone to create a roof. Then build a three-layer clay structure on top, as shown. On top of that, craft a viewing tower from stone, stone brick stair and gray stained glass, as shown.

STEP 12

On top of your roof, build a pyramid from stone brick stair. Add a 20-block emerald column on top surrounded by three rings of green stained glass for decoration and your sky fortress is complete!

Now it's time to plot the next step in your Minecraft world domination!

SKYSCRAPER

DIFFICULTY
MASTER

BUILD TIME
3 HOURS +

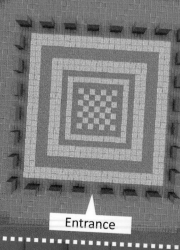

The centerpiece of many cities is often the tallest tower. This skyscraper should inspire you to create more brilliant buildings around it and establish your own metropolis. Starting with a carefully laid floor design, it finishes with a rooftop that will leave your head in the clouds.

MATERIALS

STEP 1

Build a 7x7 checkerboard from andesite and quartz block. Surround it with single rings of andesite and quartz, followed by double rings of quartz, andesite, quartz again, and stone brick. Then add five rings of polished andesite, removing blocks from each corner, as shown, before enclosing it with one final ring of stone brick.

STEP 2

Along the edges of your stone-brick square, alternate stone brick and andesite columns with gaps. Columns and gaps should be two blocks wide, apart from one column (shown here in the bottom right corner), which will only be one block wide to allow a gap of three blocks for your entrance.

Entrance

STEP 3

Add stone brick blocks to the top of your columns. Then glaze the space between each column with gray stained glass. Now you have a solid base for your skyscraper.

STEP 4

Now for the entrance! Build two columns of cobblestone wall three blocks high. Then add a row of stone brick stair on top with a 5x2 stone-brick-block rectangle behind, as shown. Make your mark on this entrance with some carpet, plants, or banners.

STEP 5

Build two columns of andesite at each corner and build the walls up so your building is six blocks high. Five blocks up, build an overhang using polished andesite slab, as shown. As your skyscraper grows, each overhang will mark a new level, or floor.

STEP 6

On the same level as your overhang, lay a floor of white hardened clay inside the skyscraper. Keep on building up following this pattern to add another 12 levels (or more!) to your skyscraper. In each corner, build a column of cobblestone wall between the andesite columns to complement the entrance.

EXPERT TIP!

PART 1: GOING UP?

Why not add an elevator to your skyscraper? First punch a 2x2 hole through the center of each floor (at ground level make this hole three blocks deep). Build an eight-block glass base into the center of the floor on the ground floor, as shown.

Replace the inner edge of polished andesite with stone brick and add another layer of white-hardened-clay flooring. Build four columns from polished andesite, stone brick and cobblestone wall. Make these columns eight blocks high.

STEP 7

Start your top floor with two layers of polished andesite slabs. The first needs to be five blocks wide and the next four blocks wide. Fill in the floor with white hardened clay, leaving space for a 5x5 glowstone square in the center to provide light.

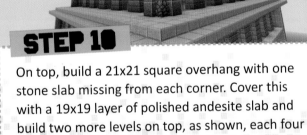

STEP 9

Build walls between each column using stone brick and gray stained glass. The central window on each side should be three blocks wide and the other four windows should be two blocks wide. Build a top rim of stone brick, as shown.

STEP 10

On top, build a 21x21 square overhang with one stone slab missing from each corner. Cover this with a 19x19 layer of polished andesite slab and build two more levels on top, as shown, each four blocks high with an overhang between them.

STEP 11

Build an overhang of stone slab then add a 21x21 layer of polished andesite slab on top. Next, add a 19x19 roof of stone brick slab and white hardened clay, like the one shown.

STEP 12

Build columns around the edges of the hardened clay square. The corner and middle columns should be one block wide, and the rest two blocks wide, as shown.

STEP 13

Build your columns four blocks high and add a rim one block high on top of them. Glaze the gaps with gray stained glass to create the final windows in your skyscraper.

STEP 14

Top this with a roof of white hardened clay surrounded by a stone brick slab rim, as shown. You're really going up in the Minecraft world now!

EXPERT TIP!

PART 2: GOING UP?

Mark each floor by replacing six floor blocks with glass, as shown in Part 1. Build stone brick blocks on top of three of the glass bases from floor to ceiling, leaving an entrance gap on one side. Pour water into the top of the elevator to make it work. Then step into the elevator to go down and press the space bar to move up again.

STEP 15

Build walls from polished andesite three blocks high and top with a stone brick and polished andesite roof. Then add three cuboids, each smaller than the last, finishing off with a tall, thin one to make your skyscraper as high as possible. As you can see, your head is quite literally in the clouds by the time your Minecraft work is done!

Now the only thing you have to decide is how to decorate and furnish your penthouse apartment!

GLOSSARY

The world of Minecraft is one that comes with its own set of special words. Here are just some of them.

《 BIOME 》

A region in a Minecraft world with special geographical features, plants, and weather conditions. There are forest, jungle, desert, and snow biomes, and each one contains different resources and numbers of mobs.

《 COLUMN 》

A series of blocks placed on top of each other.

《 DIAGONAL 》

A line of blocks joined corner to corner that looks like a staircase.

《 HOTBAR 》

The selection bar at the bottom of the screen, where you put your most useful items for easy access during Survival mode.

《 INVENTORY 》

This is a pop-up menu containing tools, blocks and other Minecraft items.

《 MOB 》

Short for "mobile," a mob is a moving Minecraft creature with special behaviors. Villagers, animals, and monsters are all mobs, and they can be friendly, like sheep and pigs, or hostile, like creepers. All spawn or breed and some — like wolves and horses — are tamable.

《 ROW 》

A horizontal line of blocks.

FURTHER INFORMATION

BOOKS

Minecraft: Guide to Creative by Mojang AB and The Official
Minecraft Team. Del Rey, 2017.

Minecraft: Guide to Exploration by Mojang AB and The Official
Minecraft Team. Del Ray, 2017.

Minecraft: The Complete Handbook Collection by Stephanie Mitton
and Paul Soares Jr. Scholastic, 2015.

WEBSITES

Visit the official Minecraft website to get started!
https://minecraft.net/en-us/

Explore over 600 kid-friendly Minecraft videos
at this awesome site!
https://www.cleanminecraftvideos.com

INDEX